SPEED RACER ™

Race for Revenge

GROSSET & DUNLAP
Published by the Penguin Group
Penguin Group (USA) Inc., 375 Hudson Street,
New York, New York 10014, USA
Penguin Group (Canada), 90 Eglinton Avenue East,
Suite 700, Toronto, Ontario M4P 2Y3, Canada
(a division of Pearson Penguin Canada Inc.)
Penguin Books Ltd., 80 Strand, London WC2R 0RL, England
Penguin Group Ireland, 25 St. Stephen's Green, Dublin 2, Ireland
(a division of Penguin Books Ltd.)
Penguin Group (Australia), 250 Camberwell Road,
Camberwell, Victoria 3124, Australia
(a division of Pearson Australia Group Pty. Ltd.)
Penguin Books India Pvt. Ltd., 11 Community Centre,
Panchsheel Park, New Delhi—110 017, India
Penguin Group (NZ), 67 Apollo Drive, Rosedale,
North Shore 0632, New Zealand
(a division of Pearson New Zealand Ltd.)
Penguin Books (South Africa) (Pty.) Ltd., 24 Sturdee Avenue,
Rosebank, Johannesburg 2196, South Africa

Penguin Books Ltd., Registered Offices:
80 Strand, London WC2R 0RL, England

The publisher does not have any control over and does not assume any
responsibility for author or third-party websites or their content.

www.speedracer.com

Designed by Michelle Martinez Design, Inc.

Library of Congress Control Number: 2007039824

ISBN 978-0-448-44809-1   10 9 8 7 6 5 4 3 2 1

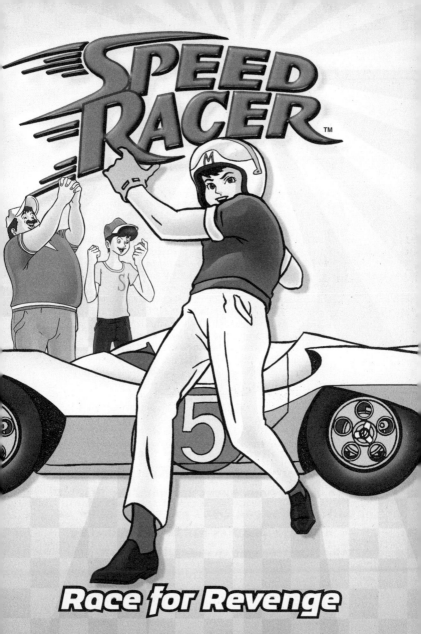

SPEED RACER™

Race for Revenge

by Chase Wheeler   Grosset & Dunlap

The Marvels of the Mach 5

The Mach 5 is one of the most
powerful and amazing racing cars in
the world. Pops Racer designed the Mach 5
with features you won't see on any other car.
All of the features can be controlled by
buttons on the steering wheel.

This button releases powerful jacks to boost the car so Sparky, the mechanic, can quickly make any necessary repairs or adjustments.

Press this button and the Mach 5 sprouts special grip tires for traction over any terrain. At the same time, an incredible 5,000 torque of horsepower is distributed equally to each wheel by auxiliary engines.

For use when Speed Racer has to race over heavily wooded terrain, powerful rotary saws protrude from the front of the Mach 5 to slash and cut any and all obstacles.

Pressing the D button releases a powerful deflector that seals the cockpit into an air-conditioned, crash and bulletproof, watertight chamber. Inside it, Speed Racer is completely isolated and shielded.

The button for special illumination allows Speed Racer to see much farther and more clearly than with ordinary headlights. It's invaluable in some of the weird and dangerous places he races the Mach 5.

Press this button when the Mach 5 is underwater. First the cockpit is supplied with oxygen, then a periscope is raised to scan the surface of the water. Everything that is seen is relayed down to the cockpit by television.

This releases a homing robot from the front of the car. The homing robot can carry pictures or tape-recorded messages to anyone or anywhere Speed Racer wants.

Speed Racer shifted down for turn one. The powerful engine of the Mach 5 moaned as he released the clutch. The tires screamed in protest as the race car drifted high on the steeply-banked curve.

So far, so good. The Mach 5 was tracking perfectly, holding its line. Speed smiled with pure pleasure as he floored the accelerator and roared out of the turn, down the long straightaway.

As he shifted up to gain speed, Speed checked his rearview mirror out of long habit. There were no cars behind him.

Did this mean Speed was running last? Hardly. There were no cars in front of him, either. The sleek Mach 5 was alone on the racetrack.

This was a practice session, and Speed was racing against time. The track was deserted and so were the stands, which were usually filled with thousands of cheering fans.

Today, only two people were watching. Both were racing fans. One was Sparky, Speed's best friend and top mechanic. The other was his girlfriend, Trixie.

"Forty-four seconds—average speed 180!" said Sparky, consulting his watch. He wore a red baseball cap and a wide smile.

"The new engine is making the Mach 5 much faster!" said Trixie, clapping her hands.

"It sure is," agreed Sparky. "And now Speed has a good chance of winning the race at Danger Pass."

They both cheered as Speed raced past in a blur. "Go, Speed Racer!" they shouted.

Sparky was proud. Even though he was young, like Speed and Trixie, he was an experienced mechanic—responsible for tuning the engine of the Mach 5.

"Speed is the best," said Trixie. Her eyes were glowing with excitement and pride.

"And he has the best car," Sparky added.

The Mach 5 had been designed and built by Speed's father, Pops Racer. It had the engine and suspension of a true racing thoroughbred. And it had lots of secret features that other race cars didn't have.

Features that would come in handy in the dangerous days ahead!

Down on the track, Speed executed another turn. His tires screamed, gripping the asphalt. Speed loved the competition of racing, where he was always running against the pack. But it was even more fun racing alone, against time, where he didn't have to worry about sharing the track with the other cars.

Suddenly, he saw a shape in his rearview mirror.

There was another car on the track, and it was coming up fast!

"Huh?" Speed floored the accelerator, but the other car was still gaining on him.

It came out of the turn, a black shape growing larger and larger in his rearview mirror.

It was catching up with him, even though he was going almost 180 miles per hour!

Speed's racing instincts took over. He edged to the right to keep the car from passing him. Speed hated to be passed!

The strange car dodged left, and Speed edged

left to block him. He grinned with pleasure. "So," he cried, "you want to play!"

The answer was a sudden jolt as the strange car clipped the Mach 5's rear fender.

Speed frowned. An accident, or a threat? He looked in the rearview mirror and saw two glowing eyes under a metal helmet shaped like a pirate hat. He saw what looked like an evil grin.

Suddenly, the strange car lunged forward to ram the Mach 5. Just as it was about to hit, Speed pressed a button on his steering wheel. The Mach 5's special auto jacks lifted it off its wheels, into the air, just in time.

The mystery car passed underneath with inches to spare.

Up in the stands, Trixie and Sparky saw it all.

"Close call!" breathed Trixie. "Where did that car come from?"

"It sure was fast," said Sparky, checking his watch. He did a few quick calculations in his head. "It went more than 220 mph!"

They both ran down to the track to meet Speed, who had pulled up in the pit. He was already pulling off his safety helmet.

"Oh, Speed, you're safe!" said Trixie.

"No thanks to him," muttered Speed angrily.

"That was a close call," said Sparky. "Where did that black race car come from?"

"I don't know," said Speed. "But the man behind the wheel is a reckless driver. He almost caused me to crash!"

Sparky nodded in agreement. "If that car is in the race at Danger Pass, you'll have to be extra careful!"

"You're right," said Speed. He remembered the glowing eyes and spooky smile of the driver. "I think that car means bad luck. I hope it's not for me!"

After midnight, it gets quiet in the city. Even the criminals go to bed. The last thing Mr. Black expected was trouble.

He had worked late, very late, and he was tired. He was driving home from his office at the Racing Car Association. He was glad to see that there was no traffic.

Suddenly he saw lights in his rearview mirror. They got brighter and brighter, coming up fast. As they got closer, he could see that it was a black race car. But what was a race car doing on the city streets?

The race car came closer, and Mr. Black saw a number flashing on the front:

X-3!

Mr. Black shivered with sudden fear. His hands gripped the wheel in terror.

He stepped on the gas, but the strange car kept coming, faster and faster.

"Can that really be the X-3?" he muttered.

As if in answer to his thoughts, a strange, ghostly voice came from the race car:

"The Mélange still races!"

"No!" said Mr. Black. "I can hear his voice!"

The race car whipped right past him. Then it did a sudden U-turn and sped back toward him. In a matter of seconds, they would have a head-on collision!

"*AAAH!*" Mr. Black cried as the race car

rammed his front bumper, flipping his sedan into the air.

The race car sped off unharmed as Mr. Black's sedan crashed through the concrete guardrail and burst into flames.

Luckily, Mr. Black jumped out just in time to save his life. As he crawled from the wreckage, Mr. Black could still hear the ghostly voice, taunting him as the black race car sped away.

"The Mélange still races . . ."

And he saw a scrap of paper drifting down from the roadway above. On it were two letters:

X-3.

The next morning, Speed got a phone call. "It's for you," said Pops Racer, handing Speed the telephone. They were in the Racer family shop, working on the Mach 5.

Pops looked at his son suspiciously. "Who was that?" he asked when Speed hung up the phone.

"It was Inspector Detector," said Speed, hurrying out. "I'm wanted at police headquarters."

Speed hurried downtown. He was always eager and willing to help the police in their efforts to fight crime. He found Inspector Detector waiting in his office. A racing official was also there.

Inspector Detector was investigating a strange accident from the night before, and he wanted their help.

"A racing official, Mr. Black, was run off the

road and almost killed last night," he said. "By a strange race car."

"A race car?" exclaimed Speed.

Inspector Detector described the incident.

"Hmmm! It sounds like the strange car I saw at the track yesterday," said Speed. "The driver was reckless and dangerous!"

Inspector Detector twirled the ends of his black beard with his fingertips. He always did that when he was thinking.

"But Speed, Mr. Herring here of the Racing Car Association claims that he's neither seen nor heard of such a car," he said. "It makes the case even more puzzling."

"It's important, Inspector, that you catch this wild driver immediately, before he causes even worse accidents!" Mr. Herring said.

"I agree," said Inspector Detector. "And we're doing the best we can. In fact, we already have a clue!"

Mr. Herring looked surprised. "You have?

What is it?" he asked.

"It was found at the scene of the accident," said Inspector Detector. He pulled a sheet of paper from his coat pocket. It was marked *X-3*.

"Here it is, Mr. Herring. What do you make of it?"

Mr. Herring broke into a sweat. He looked as if he had seen a ghost. "Why, uh," he said nervously. "It seems to be only a card."

"Do the letters X-3 mean anything to you, Mr. Herring?"

Speed could tell that the older man wasn't telling the truth. He was hiding something. But what? And why?

"Uh, let me see," Herring said. "Uh, no, sir. I can't tell you a thing!"

"That's too bad," said Inspector Detector. "I was hoping you might recognize it as a race car number." He folded the paper and put it away. "However, rest assured, we will conduct a thorough investigation and bring that driver to justice."

Mr. Herring stood up and put on his hat. Speed noticed that his hands were shaking. "I'm sure you will, Inspector Detector. Now, I have important business, so if you will excuse me."

He hurried out the door.

Downstairs, Mr. Herring got into his car and hurriedly dialed his cell phone. He looked worried.

His fingers were shaking as he dialed.

Miles away, in a huge mansion overlooking

the sea, another racing official had been pacing impatiently when he answered his phone.

"Green here, who's this? Herring! What do you want?"

Mr. Green scowled as he listened.

"What do you mean the accident was caused by Marker's car? The X-3? That's not possible!"

Mr. Green scowled even more at the answer.

"Forget it, Herring. It's not possible. Now, I have work to do."

Mr. Green hung up. And scowled again.

"Impossible!" he said. "Believing in ghosts!"

Later that night, a midnight blue sedan sped along a narrow road overlooking an ocean cliff. At the wheel was the same Mr. Green who had taken the phone call from Herring.

He saw headlights behind him. He sped up impatiently. He was a racing official, and he didn't like to be passed. The blue sedan whipped around the narrow curves, faster and faster.

The car drew closer. It was catching up.

BEEP! BEEP! came the eerie sound of a horn.

Mr. Green looked in the mirror and saw the markings on the front of the car:

X-3!

He broke into a sweat and his hands gripped the steering wheel. He jammed the accelerator to the floor.

"Can that really be the X-3?" he muttered.

As if in answer, a spooky voice rose above the sound of the racing engines.

"The Mélange still races!"

"No! I can hear his voice!" said Mr. Green, his eyes fixed on the car in his rearview mirror.

The strange race car pulled out to pass, then edged closer and closer to Mr. Green's sedan. The driver had glowing eyes and he was grinning.

Mr. Green tried to brake, but it was too late. He was trapped between the race car and the guardrail.

Then, with a sudden turn, he was forced off the road, through the guardrail—

And into the ocean below!

CRASH!

As Mr. Green swam to the surface, he saw the car that had wrecked him disappear into the night.

He heard a voice: "The Mélange still races . . ."

And he saw a scrap of paper fluttering down through the air. As it twisted and turned, closer and closer, he was able to read what was written on it:

X-3.

The next day was beautiful and sunny. Speed was busy waxing the elegant lines of the Mach 5, getting ready for the big race at Danger Pass. It was only a few days away.

He listened to the radio as he worked. All the news was about the recent accidents:

"Inspector Detector of the municipal police has set up a special team to catch the mysterious race car that roars away from the scene of accidents, leaving only a card that says X-3."

"I wish I could be part of that team," said Speed thoughtfully.

Just then, out of the corner of his eye, he saw a delicate hand reach into the car to turn off the radio.

Speed looked around, startled.

It was Trixie. She had a picnic hamper.

"Sorry I kept you waiting, Speed," she said. "But I was making a picnic lunch for us. Isn't it the most beautiful day for a drive in the country?"

"Uh, I suppose," stammered Speed. He had forgotten all about their plans! He was too busy thinking about the recent accidents.

Trixie was smiling, looking especially pretty in her summer outfit.

"Oh, Speed, may I have the key to the trunk?" she asked.

Speed tossed her the keys absentmindedly. *Why are racing officials being attacked?* he wondered. *And what does X-3 stand for?*

After stowing the picnic lunch in the trunk, Trixie got into the Mach 5, smoothing her skirt over her knees.

"We start in five seconds," she said, laughingly. She could tell that Speed was distracted, but she knew how to get his attention.

"All drivers get behind their wheels," she said, trying to sound like a racing announcer.

Speed laughed and jumped into the Mach 5 beside her. "Didn't take me long when you said it like that, did it, Trixie?" he said, laughing. He loved Trixie's humor. Now he was looking forward to their day together.

Just then, a police squad car pulled up beside the Mach 5. It was Inspector Detector. He got out of the squad car, waving his hands excitedly. His black beard was blowing in the breeze like a flag.

"Oh, Speed," he said. "Don't go yet. I've got to ask you to do the police department a favor!"

Trixie groaned. A frown settled on her pretty features.

"We need you to help us in the investigation of that mysterious race car that is causing all the accidents," said Inspector Detector.

Speed was all ears.

"As you know, that car is amazingly fast," Inspector Detector said. "And frankly, our squad cars can't catch up with it."

"You've spotted it, then?" Speed asked.

Inspector Detector was just about to answer when Trixie spoke up.

"I'm sorry, Inspector," she said in a sweet but stern voice. "But Speed already has a very important appointment today."

Speed didn't want to disappoint his girlfriend, but he knew he had to help Inspector Detector.

"We can go for our drive in the country next week, Trixie. Okay?"

Trixie didn't answer. She folded her arms and pouted.

"Will you help us, Speed?" Inspector Detector pleaded.

"A fine police department we have," said Trixie, "when they have to ask for *your* help on the day we were going on a picnic!"

"Now, you know, Trixie, it's our duty to help!" Speed was adamant. "We'll go on the picnic next week instead."

"Humph!" Trixie said. "I spent all last night making a special lunch. What's going to happen to that?"

Suddenly a tiny voice was heard. "Don't worry, I'll eat it!"

They all looked around.

Speed's little brother, Spritle, was standing

behind the Mach 5 with his pet chimpanzee, Chim Chim. They both wore identical red and white striped hats.

"Chim Chim and I are ready to investigate the case, Inspector Detector!" said Spritle. "Do you see what Chim Chim is carrying?"

The little chimp was wearing a backpack. He jumped up and down excitedly.

"It looks to me like some kind of recorder," said Speed. It had a microphone and a reel for tape.

Spritle shook his head. "But it's cleverly disguised," he said, sounding disappointed that Speed could see what it was. "Doesn't it look more like a camera?"

It didn't look at all like a camera to Speed. But he decided to play along with his little brother's game.

"You're right. It looks like a camera," he said.

"What's it for?" asked Trixie.

"It's to fool spies!" said Spritle, growing more

and more excited.

Spies? thought Speed. "But if there are no spies in this case, what are you going to tape-record?"

"Hmmm," said Spritle. He scratched his head thoughtfully. "Then maybe I'll just record Chim Chim!"

"*Hoo-haa!*" said Chim Chim, scratching his head, too.

They all laughed, even Inspector Detector. Speed's mischievous little brother was always good for a laugh.

Just then, a stern voice broke into their laughter. It came from the police radio in Inspector Detector's squad car:

"The mysterious race car has been spotted! It's traveling south on Highway 5 at 180 miles per hour and the police are unable to catch up to it!"

That was all Speed needed to hear.

"I'll go!" he said, strapping on his seat belt. He turned the key and the Mach 5's mighty engine roared to life.

"Thank you, Speed!" said Inspector Detector as he ran for his squad car.

Trixie began to fasten her seat belt, but Speed stopped her with one hand.

"I have to do this alone," he said.

"What about me?" Trixie asked. "Aren't you going to take me?"

"It's too dangerous, Trixie," said Speed. He reached across her and opened the car door. "Get out now, please! Hurry!"

Trixie got out of the Mach 5 and watched as Speed Racer roared off to join the chase. She

managed a tiny, feeble wave.

No picnic! No ride in the country! This was what it was like to be Speed Racer's girlfriend.

Here she was, left behind again, with Speed's little brother and his chimp.

Then she looked around.

She was alone. "What happened to Spritle and Chim Chim?" she said. "I wonder where they could be?"

It was the car chase of the century!

Four powerful police squad cars, their engines straining, were running at full speed, trying to catch the mysterious black race car.

Their lights were flashing, alerting pedestrians to get out of the way. Their sirens were blasting, clearing the intersections ahead.

But still, they were falling behind.

The mysterious black race car was too powerful, too fast.

Then a sleek white racer with an *M* on the front and a 5 on the side caught up with the police cars. Without slowing, it wove through their formation like a flash of lightning streaking through a cloud.

It was Speed Racer in the Mach 5. The mighty engine purred powerfully. The tires were humming along. Speed felt the thrill of the chase as he gunned the Mach 5 through the slower squad cars, leaving them behind.

As soon as he was in the open, he floored the gas pedal.

The Mach 5 sprang ahead like a deer, and the chase was on.

175, 180, 190 mph.

The mysterious car spun up an expressway ramp toward the city center, heedless of the dangers involved.

"Uh-oh!" cried Speed. "He's going to kill somebody!" He sped up the ramp after him.

In the city, people crossing the streets heard a menacing sound. They scattered as the black race car careened through the narrow streets, scattering pedestrians and cars alike.

"I've got to stop him!" cried Speed as he followed close behind. "He has no respect for the lives of others!"

Just then the black race car plowed through a

farmers' market in the center of town. Fruits and vegetables scattered as the stalls and stands were overturned.

Luckily, no one had been hit. The black car sped off, and the people began picking up the mess.

But Speed was right behind the X-3, also running wide open! He downshifted, trying to slow the Mach 5. He jammed on his brakes, but it was too late to stop. He was just about to plow into the crowd at the farmers' market when he hit the button on his steering wheel that activated the auto jacks.

The Mach 5 was lifted into the air and sailed

over the curious crowd.

"Close call," muttered Speed as he hit the ground and renewed the chase.

Speed was gaining on the X-3. He was only a block behind the car when it disappeared around a corner. Speed took the corner on two wheels, then braked to a sudden stop in the middle of a four-way intersection.

Where had the black race car gone?

Speed looked left, then right. He looked ahead. He even looked behind. The black race car was nowhere to be seen.

The streets were empty in every direction.

"Lost him!" Speed yelled.

Then he saw a flower shop on the corner. A beautiful young woman with honey-blond hair was arranging bouquets out front.

Speed jumped out of the Mach 5 and went to ask her for help. Perhaps she had seen the car he was chasing.

"Pardon me, miss," said Speed. "But did you see a black race car pass by your shop?"

She looked at him with soft dark eyes.

"No, I'm sorry," she said. "I didn't see anything."

How could that be? Speed wondered. *How*

could she have missed it? How often do race cars speed down the city streets?

"That's peculiar," he said. "I wonder what could have happened to the car?"

She ignored his question and went back to her task, arranging flowers.

She's almost as lovely as these flowers are, thought Speed. *And every bit as mysterious!*

He went back to the Mach 5, which was parked in the middle of the intersection. Inspector Detector, who had been following at a distance, pulled up in his squad car.

Speed pointed over his shoulder at the shop. "According to the girl in the flower shop, the race car we were chasing didn't pass by here."

Inspector Detector pulled at his beard. "Strange," he said. "It must have made a lot of noise."

"I only lost sight of it for a few seconds," said Speed. "Somehow it disappeared, right here in this intersection."

They both looked to the right and the left. Empty streets in all directions, and no sign of the mysterious black race car.

"I'm sorry, but I've let you down again, Inspector Detector," said Speed. "I let that car get away from me."

Inspector Detector clapped him on the shoulder and managed a smile.

"It's all right, Speed," he said. "I've ordered roadblocks, so pretty soon someone should report seeing it again."

"I sure hope so," said Speed. He was anxious to get back in the chase. Just then, he heard the two-way radio on the Mach 5:

"Calling Speed Racer in the Mach 5. Speed! Calling Speed Racer in the Mach 5!"

"That's Trixie calling," he cried as he ran toward the car.

"Calling Speed!" Trixie's voice on the radio sounded far away. "The mysterious race car just passed the intersection three blocks north of your

present location."

Where is she? How does she know? Speed wondered.

Then he heard the familiar sound of a helicopter overhead. Trixie had been following him in her personal helicopter! Unlike most girls her age, she was an excellent helicopter pilot.

Speed waved back, and then picked up the mike for the two-way radio. "This is the Mach 5, Trixie! Thanks for spotting him!"

Trixie laughed. "I've got to help," she said. "Because if you don't catch him, we won't be able to go on our picnic next week, either."

"Roger that," said Speed. "I'm after him!"

He turned the key and the Mach 5's engine roared to life.

"By the way," asked Trixie, trying not to sound jealous, "who was that girl I saw you talking to?"

But Speed didn't hear her question. He was already on his way, and the roar of the engine drowned her out.

It also drowned out the sounds of Spritle and Chim Chim hiding in the trunk. They were laughing and chattering as they enjoyed the picnic lunch Trixie had made!

Speed Racer got to the intersection just in time to see the mysterious race car speeding out of town on a narrow country road.

He downshifted and followed at 180 mph. It took all his skill to stay on the road. The car he was chasing was amazingly fast!

Ahead, Speed saw a railroad crossing. The lights were flashing and the bar was coming down. A train was approaching!

"Good! He'll have to stop," said Speed. "Now I've got him!"

But instead of stopping, the mysterious race car kept going. It sped through the railroad crossing, just in front of the train, just under the lowering crossbar.

But the bar caught the driver and yanked him out of the driver's seat. Amazingly, the car kept going with no driver.

Speed slammed on his brakes and the Mach 5 skidded to a stop. He jumped out and ran to the lowered crossbar to see if the driver was all right.

The driver was hanging on it like a rag doll.

"Gotcha!" said Speed, grabbing him and pulling him back. He could hardly wait to look his adversary in the eye!

But when he turned the driver's head, all he saw was a metal mask with two holes for eyes and a grinning slot for a mouth.

"The Mélange still . . ." it whispered.

Its final words were lost in the roar of the passing train.

Then the eyes blinked out, and all was silent.

As the Mach 5 pulled into the garage at police headquarters, Trixie was landing her helicopter on the roof. She joined Speed and helped him carry the mystery race car's "driver" into Inspector Detector's office.

They laid it on a table and looked at it in amazement.

"It's a robot!" said Inspector Detector. "This means that the black race car was being operated by remote control!"

"I'm sorry, Inspector," said Speed, "that the black race car was able to get away from me!"

"You did a good job, anyway, Speed, in bringing back this robot. By analyzing the robot's mechanisms, we'll be able to learn something about whoever made it."

He pulled at his beard thoughtfully as he

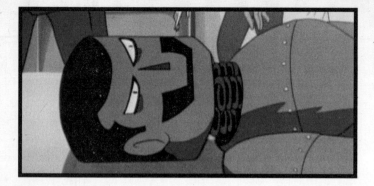

examined the robot. Speed and Trixie looked on. The robot's neck was made of springs and the hands were just metal claws.

The mouth was just a slot in the shape of an evil grin.

"Oh, I almost forgot!" said Speed. "The robot said something!"

"It did?" Inspector Detector looked hopeful. "What did it say?"

Speed shook his head. "The train made so much noise as it was going by that I wasn't able to make it out."

A small voice broke in. "I tape-recorded what it said!"

Trixie and Speed both looked down. "Spritle!"

The mischievous little boy and his chimp climbed out from under Inspector Detector's desk. Both were wearing silly grins.

"I got it all!" said Spritle, patting the machine Chim Chim was holding. "I recorded the whole thing!"

"You were hiding in the Mach 5 again!" said Trixie. She glared at him. Speed's little brother was cute, but he could be annoying, too.

"Right!" said Spritle.

"Hoo-haa," agreed Chim Chim.

"Oh, Spritle, you might have been hurt!" said

Trixie, placing her hands on her hips to show that she was serious.

"Well, I got a tape recording!"

"And I suppose you ate our picnic lunch, too," said Speed.

Spritle nodded. Chim Chim nodded, too.

Trixie shook her head disapprovingly. "Then give the tape recording to Inspector Detector so he can hear it," she said.

She reached for the recorder.

"Uh-oh! Not so fast," said Spritle, jumping in front of Chim Chim. "Will you give us some cake if we let you listen to it?"

"You'll get cake later," Inspector Detector said sternly. He'd had enough of Spritle's nonsense. "Let me listen to that recording right now!"

"What about our cake?" demanded Spritle.

"As soon as this case is solved, I'll buy you a seven-layer chocolate cake," said Inspector Detector.

Spritle grabbed the tape recorder and handed

it to Inspector Detector. "Here!"

It was a deal! They laughed at the mischievous pair. Boys and chimps want to have fun.

But it was time to get serious.

Inspector Detector set the recorder on his desk and pressed PLAY. Silence fell over the room as they listened to the spooky voice:

"The Mélange still . . ."

Inspector Detector rewound it and played it again.

"The Mélange still . . . the Mélange still . . ."

Inspector Detector turned off the tape recorder, looking puzzled. He pulled at his black beard thoughtfully.

"Mélange? What's Mélange? Does anyone know what that means?"

"Hmmm!" It *did* sound familiar to Speed. He searched his memory. Then he said, "Mélange is the name of a famous horse!"

"What? A horse? A race horse?"

"Not exactly, Inspector," said Speed. "I read all about Mélange when I was studying history. I remember that Napoleon had a horse by that name. It was a great horse and once it saved Napoleon's life."

Trixie looked at her boyfriend admiringly. He was not only a great race driver, he was good at history, too!

But Inspector Detector was not so impressed.

"Well, that's very interesting, Speed, but what's the connection? What does Napoleon's horse have to do with this case?"

"Yeah, tell us," said Trixie. Even though she was proud of Speed's historical knowledge, she was wondering the same thing.

Speed Racer shrugged helplessly. "Beats me," he said.

Just then the door opened, and a deep voice said, "Maybe I can tell you!"

"Pops!" said Speed.

Pops Racer walked though Inspector Detector's door. Pops had been a wrestler before he had started designing and building race cars. He still looked the part.

"There was once another Mélange," he said.

"I'd like to hear about it, Mr. Racer," said Inspector Detector.

Pops nodded, and they all sat down to listen. Even Spritle and Chim Chim!

"You all know the big race at Danger Pass is coming up," said Pops. "Well, about fifteen years ago, another race was held at Danger Pass, over one of the most difficult race courses in the world. The same Mr. Black and Mr. Green who were recently wrecked by the mysterious black race car were coaching a race team that was expected to

win. The Three Roses racing team."

"Hmmm," said Inspector Detector, pulling at his beard.

"But they were worried that they might be beaten by a young racer named Flash Marker. He was driving car number X-3, which he called the Mélange."

"X-3!" said Speed, remembering the cards that the dangerous race car had left behind.

"There were fifty cars in the race, and for the first half it looked as if it could be won by anybody. But then Flash Marker started passing all the other cars. His Mélange had a special supercharged engine. Flash was about to take the lead at the top of Danger Pass when another car cut in front of him, and he spun out. He crashed through the guardrail and fell into the valley far below. That was the end of Flash Marker, and of the Mélange."

"Oh, dear!" said Trixie. She hated to think that something like that might happen to Speed someday.

"That's quite a story, Pops," said Speed. "Inspector, don't you think it must have something to do with the case we're working on?"

"There seems to be a connection, all right," said Inspector Detector. "Pops, in that race at Danger Pass years ago, was Flash Marker wrecked on purpose, or was it accidental?"

"No one ever found out for sure," said Pops Racer. "All I know is that one of the Three Roses cars was responsible."

"Hmmm," said Inspector Detector. "I believe Mr. Herring of the Racing Car Association is coaching their team this year."

"Maybe that's why he seemed so nervous," said Speed.

"What a sad story," said Trixie. "Did Flash Marker leave any family behind?"

"Well, I seem to remember that he had children, just like me," said Pops Racer, putting his arms around Speed and Spritle. "Except that his kids were a boy and a girl."

"Wonder what happened to them," said Inspector Detector. "Are they involved in racing?"

"I doubt it," said Pops Racer. "I think the daughter runs a little flower shop downtown."

"I think I know her!" said Speed.

Trixie shot him a jealous look, but Speed ignored her. "Let's head downtown!" he said.

A little while later, the Mach 5 and Inspector Detector's squad car pulled up in front of the flower shop.

The pretty girl with the honey-blond hair was arranging flowers out front.

"Hello, Miss Marker," said Speed. "I believe we have met before."

"I remember," she said in a sweet, soft voice. "Would you like to buy some flowers?"

"No, thank you," said Speed. "My name is Speed Racer, and . . ."

Trixie interrupted, stepping between them.

"And my name is Trixie!" she said, placing her hand on Speed's shoulder. "I'm Speed's girlfriend!"

Trixie wanted to make sure that this flower girl knew that Speed was off-limits.

Inspector Detector stepped forward and introduced himself. "You must be Lily Marker," he said. "I believe your brother is Flash Marker Junior. Is he here?"

"Yes, he is, Inspector. We live at the back of the store. But my brother Flash is sick in bed."

"I'm sorry to hear that, Miss Marker, but I'd like to speak with him, just for a moment, if I may. It's official police business."

"All right," Lily said. "Come this way."

She seems troubled, thought Speed. *I wonder why?*

Speed, Trixie, and Inspector Detector followed Lily through the flower shop to a small bedroom in back.

A young man with stringy hair lay in the bed with the covers pulled up to his chin. He opened one eye and glared at his visitors.

"Flash hasn't been well," said Lily. "He's been in bed for three weeks now."

Inspector Detector pulled at his beard. "So, he's been in bed all day today?"

Lily nodded. Flash Junior scowled but didn't say anything.

"We're investigating a mysterious race car that has caused some bad accidents lately," said

Inspector Detector. "Do you know anything about it, Flash?"

Flash shook his head.

"Are you certain?"

Flash scowled and nodded.

"Well, then, thank you for your time," said Inspector Detector.

He left, and Trixie followed. Speed paused in the doorway and looked back at the scowling young man in the bed.

"There's something suspicious about him," he muttered to himself. "Something dangerous!"

Moments later, Lily stood on the sidewalk, watching Speed and Trixie drive away. They were following Inspector Detector's squad car.

As soon as the cars were out of sight, Lily heard an evil laugh behind her.

She turned and saw her brother standing in the flower shop door, leaning on a crutch.

"Hahaha!" he laughed again. It was a wicked, ugly laugh. "The cops were unable to find out

anything, thanks to you, Lily!"

Lily burst into tears. "Oh, Flash, you told me to lie, and I did it to save you. But I can't lie anymore." She wrung her hands in desperation.

"Get over it, Lily," said Flash. "We have a job to do."

Lily grabbed his arm and pleaded. "Oh, please, Flash, you've got to stop driving that car!"

"Don't worry, Lily. They caught the robot, so I am making some changes to the car. Changes I've been planning for years. Let me show you. Come inside."

Still sobbing, Lily followed her brother back to the bedroom behind the flower shop. He pressed a button in the wall, and the bed swung away, revealing a secret passageway.

"Come, Lily," he said. He led her down a flight of steep stairs to a huge underground garage.

Lily's eyes grew wide with amazement.

"You didn't know I'd built this secret workshop underneath your flower shop, did you, Lily?"

"No, Flash, I had no idea." The garage was enormous. It was crammed with tools and equipment. It even had a racetrack, steeply banked, around the walls.

In the center was the black race car, minus the robot driver. The windshield was broken and the body was banged up where the railroad crossbar had smashed into it.

"That black race car was just for practice, Lily," said Flash. He grinned. "Watch this."

He picked up a remote control and pressed a button.

A hook lowered from the ceiling and lifted the dented body off the race car's chassis. Then it lowered a new body, a sleek, familiar-looking one.

"Our father's car!" exclaimed Lily.

"The Mélange," said Flash. "I have restored and rebuilt it for the big race at Danger Pass. I can't drive it with this bad leg, but you can!"

"Me?" Lily shrunk back, frightened. "No, Flash. I can't. I won't."

"You have to, Lily. The car has to have a driver to enter the race. But I will be operating it from a helicopter above with this remote control." He showed her the remote in his hand.

"No!"

"Yes! I need you. Now get behind the wheel."

Flash pushed her into the driver's seat, then started the car by remote control. He pushed the joystick forward and the car took off around the track, going faster and faster.

"No!" said Lily. "Stop the car!" She tried to get out, but the car was going too fast.

"Lily, have you forgotten that the Mélange was wrecked by the Three Roses team? We lost our father because they cared more for winning than they did for his life!"

Lily sobbed.

"I'll get even with them for what they did to our father! I'll get revenge!"

Flash pressed the joystick forward. The car went faster and faster around the tiny track.

"No, please, Flash! Forget what happened to our father!"

"I can't. They're going to pay for what they did to him!"

Flash stood in the center of the cave, operating the car with the remote. As she sped by, holding on for dear life, Lily saw big tears running down her brother's face.

"Promise me, Lily. Promise me you will ride in the Mélange in the race. That way I can destroy the Three Roses team, and we can get our revenge!"

"Flash, please, stop the car!"

"I will, but only if you will promise, Lily. After what those men did to our father, we never saw him again! Please, Lily!"

Lily saw her brother's tears. Her pity for him overcame her fear.

"I promise," she sobbed. "Even though I know it's wrong!"

Flash pulled the joystick back and the race car rolled to a stop.

He ran to the car and held his sobbing sister in his arms.

"You won't be sorry, Lily," he said. "Remember, you are doing this for our father. We are not racing to win, we are racing for revenge!"

Speed's heart was pounding.

He had been waiting and practicing for this day for months. It was the day of the biggest and most exciting road race of the year, Danger Pass!

The grandstands were filled with eager racing fans. They all cheered in anticipation as the race cars assembled in the pits below.

The loudspeaker boomed:

"Ladies and gentlemen. Let us introduce some of the world-famous drivers who will take part in the race at Danger Pass."

A hush fell over the crowd. They all had their favorite drivers. They waited to hear their names.

"Racing car number six will be driven by Skid Chill. Car number seventy-seven will be driven by Sutton Grimes. Car number eighty-six by Scootem Rooter . . ."

Loud cheers erupted as each name was announced. But the biggest cheer went up for the young man in the bright blue shirt and the red scarf.

"And the fabulous Mach 5, driven by none other than Speed Racer . . ."

Speed waved to the crowd and went back to work assisting Sparky, who was giving a few last touches to the engine of the Mach 5.

Meanwhile, all up and down the pit area, race car owners and coaches were giving final instructions to their drivers.

Mr. Herring was addressing the three drivers of the Three Roses team.

"Speed Racer has been suspicious of us ever since Black and Green were wiped out by that mysterious X-3 race car," he said. "He'll be watching for violations."

"Don't worry about a thing, Mr. Herring," said one of his drivers.

"We know how to take care of that kid," said another.

"We'll whack him!" said the third.

"Good!" Herring nodded in approval. Just then, they all looked up, alarmed, as another race car pulled into the pit area.

It was a silver car, and it looked familiar.

"Huh!?" gasped Herring.

"That car looks like the Mélange!" said one driver.

"That's the car Flash drove when we knocked him over the cliff years ago!" said another.

"That's the Mélange. I'd know it anywhere!" said the third.

All three broke into a sweat.

The loudspeaker crackled and boomed: "Racing car number three has just joined the starting lineup. It will be driven by a rookie driver, Miss Julie."

Herring smiled and relaxed. "You see? Don't worry, men! That's number three, not X-3. Besides, it's only a girl at the wheel."

The drivers all nodded.

"Just do everything you can to win," said

Herring. His eyes narrowed to two evil slits as he hissed, "Everything, understand? Everything!"

Meanwhile, Speed and Trixie were watching Sparky at work. Soon the Mach 5 would be ready to win! Then Speed heard the announcer and looked up. He saw the new entry, car number three, at the other end of the pit.

"That girl at the wheel, she looks sort of familiar," he mused. She was almost as cute as Trixie!

He studied her with a dreamy look in his eye.

Trixie slugged him on the shoulder to get his attention. "What's the matter, Speed, haven't you

ever seen a girl racer before?"

Speed didn't answer. He was staring at the pretty girl in the red helmet and goggles.

"SPEED!" Trixie yelled in his ear.

Speed waved her away. "There's something I'm trying to figure out, Trixie. But I can't."

"Hmph," said Trixie, her hands on her hips. "There's something I'm trying to figure out, too, and I *can*!"

Just then Sparky slammed the Mach 5's hood shut. "Speed, the Mach 5 is ready to go! I have re-jetted the carburetors for a high-altitude run! The rest is up to you."

"I'll do my best," said Speed. He was ready to prove that he was one of the world's best drivers, in spite of his young age.

"I'll help you with your helmet, Speed," said Trixie. "I want you to come back safely!"

Safety is an important part of every race. Trixie helped Speed fasten his seat belts and check his safety gear. Both of them were concentrating on

the race ahead. Neither of them saw Sprite and Chim Chim tiptoeing to the back of the Mach 5.

"Climb in," whispered Sprite as he opened the trunk. He wasn't about to miss the biggest and most dangerous race of the year—not if he could help it!

He and the chimp were just about to close the lid when two huge hands grabbed them and yanked them out of the trunk.

"Pops!" Sprite squealed.

"Trying to stow away again?" Pops said.

With a squirming boy under one arm and a

squealing chimp under the other, he hurried off toward the stands to watch the race.

"Wait for me!" said Sparky. He wished Speed luck and followed.

⚫ ⚫ ⚫ ⚫

Speed saw his father heading up into the stands carrying Spritle and Chim Chim. "He caught them trying to stow away!" he laughed.

"Spritle always wants to ride with you," said Trixie. "He hates to be left behind!"

Then she saw that the trunk where Spritle and Chim Chim liked to hide was still open.

And empty!

"And so do I," she whispered with a grin.

⚫ ⚫ ⚫ ⚫

Up in the stands, Pops and Sparky were getting ready to watch the race. They grinned at

each other. They knew that the Mach 5 could win, with Speed at the wheel.

Pops looked around. "What happened to Trixie?" he asked. "Isn't she going to watch the race?"

"I saw her by the car just a minute ago," said Sparky.

"Gentlemen—and lady—start your engines!" said the announcer.

The magnificent roar of fifty cars starting at once shook the stands. It sounded like a thunderstorm. It drowned out the sound of the helicopter hovering overhead.

Flash Junior was at the controls. He looked down, studying the cars lining up with an evil grin. "Today I will avenge my father. I will make them pay!"

The eyes of all the racers were on the lights at the starting line as they changed from red, to yellow, to green.

Then the green flag flew, and the cars were off! The sweet smell of raw fuel and burning rubber filled the stands.

In the stands, Pops and Sprite and Sparky cheered for their favorite:

"Go, Speed Racer!"

Chim Chim added his own cheer: *"Hoo-haa!"*

On the track, Speed relied on his razor-sharp instincts to get the Mach 5 off the line and into the first turn.

His hands were busy with the wheel and the gearshift, but his mind was on the story he had heard about Flash Marker's tragedy fifteen years before.

"The first race in years at Danger Pass," he muttered. "There's a car that looks just like the original Mélange. The Three Roses club has three cars entered. Are they planning more mischief? Is someone plotting revenge?"

Even as Speed was considering all this, the Three Roses cars were communicating by radio. Mr. Herring's orders to his drivers were grim. "Speed Racer suspects us, I'm sure. At your first opportunity, get rid of the Mach 5!"

"Okay!"

"Roger that!"

"Will do!"

Meanwhile, up above, Flash's helicopter was following the race cars as they began to negotiate the treacherous curves. Flash flew the helicopter with one hand, while with the other he used the remote to control the rebuilt Mélange.

"Lily," he said on the radio. "Keep a tight grip on the steering wheel, and no one will know that I am actually driving. It won't be long until I get my revenge! The revenge I've been planning for years!"

Pushing the joystick forward, he watched gleefully as the Mélange accelerated faster and faster.

"No, please!" cried Lily. She closed her eyes and began to sob. "No, Flash, please!"

The supercharged engine roared as the Mélange wound through the pack, dodging right and left. Lily gripped the wheel in terror as she

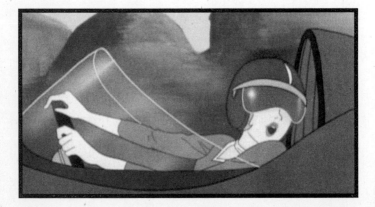

whipped past the Mach 5.

Speed Racer watched in awe as car number three passed him.

"Who is that girl behind the wheel?" he cried as he floored his accelerator and took off in pursuit. "I've got to know!"

Far above, Flash looked down and saw the Mach 5 and the Mélange, now running side by side on the road.

"Speed Racer's going to ruin it for me!" he muttered. "I've got to take care of him first, before I wipe out the Three Roses cars."

He pressed a button on his remote control. Below, a panel on the Mélange turned over. It replaced the number three with a new number:

X-3!

As Flash operated the remote control, the newly named X-3 bashed into the Mach 5's rear fender. *"Ugh!"* shouted Speed as he skillfully recovered from a deadly spin.

"No, Flash, please!" shouted Lily. She was

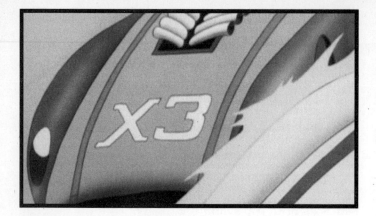

afraid of crashing. She was even more afraid of making Speed crash.

"Now we've got him, Lily!" shouted Flash into the radio as he rammed the Mélange into the Mach 5 again.

The impact knocked off Lily's helmet. Now unconscious, Lily slumped over the wheel of the speeding car.

Flash laughed with glee and edged the X-3 to the right, trying to force Speed's car off the road. Speed resisted, edging to the left.

Sparks flew from the wheels as the two cars touched. Speed fought the steering wheel, trying

to keep from going over the cliff. He glanced over at the driver who was trying to kill him.

Her eyes were closed. Her helmet had blown off and her long blond hair was blowing in the wind.

"That's Lily!" Speed cried. "And she's not driving that car!"

He looked up and saw the helicopter. So it was in control! How could he save himself without endangering Lily?

Skillfully, Speed drove the Mach 5 off the racetrack, down a long gravel slope. He cut across a switchback, then slipped back onto the track again.

There he saw that the X-3 had made a U-turn and was heading straight toward him!

Speed downshifted and threw the Mach 5 into a controlled powerslide, barely missing the other car, then escaped on a long straightaway.

"Darn!" muttered Flash, high above. "I have never seen such driving. I had better concentrate on the Three Roses cars for now. Later on, I'll see that Speed Racer gets what's coming to him!"

Meanwhile, up in the grandstands, Pops Racer was pacing up and down. He was too nervous to stay in his seat. He, Sparky, Spritle, and Chim Chim were listening to the announcer's voice over the loudspeaker:

"The first group of racers has just passed checkpoint three! Car number six is in the lead! Followed closely by number twelve and the Three Roses club cars. Average speed right now is 143.7 miles per hour."

"Hmph!" muttered Pops. "Where's Speed? Is he behind? Is he ahead?"

"Take it easy, Pops," said Sparky. "There's nothing you can do right now. The race has three more hours to go."

"Three hours?!" cried Spritle.

"Take it easy?!" Pops exclaimed. "How can you

expect me to take it easy when I'm worried about my son? I want to know how Speed is doing."

Then Pops looked around. "I wonder where Trixie is? Have you seen her, Sparky?"

Sparky shrugged and reminded him, "The last time I saw her, she was standing beside the Mach 5."

"I bet I know where she is," said Spritle.

"Huh?" said Pops. "Where?"

"In the Mach 5!" said Spritle.

At that moment, the Mach 5 was straining up the steep grade to Danger Pass.

The X-3, however, was pulling ahead. The Mach 5 was behind.

"That car is too fast," said Speed. "I can't seem to overtake it. It's an amazing car, and it might be even better than the Mach 5!"

Speed studied the tachometer to see what the problem might be. His engine speed seemed

okay. *Something else must be wrong,* he thought. Something else was holding him back.

"Feels like extra weight!" he said. Then he remembered that he sometimes had stowaways. "Maybe Spritle and Chim Chim got away from Pops," he muttered. "I'd better check the trunk!"

Speed's disk brakes glowed red as he pulled to a stop at the side of the track and jumped out of the car.

"Spritle, are you in there?" he yelled as he flung open the trunk of the Mach 5. "Come on out!"

"Sorry, but Spritle's not here, Speed," said a soft, sweet voice.

"Trixie?!" Speed gave her a hand and helped her out of the trunk. "What's the big idea?"

Trixie was cuter than ever in her red racing suit and helmet. "I want to be in a race with you," she said. "And not in the trunk, either! Spritle is welcome to ride in there all he wants."

She smiled at Speed, but he was not so easily won over. In fact, he was furious.

"Is that so? Let me warn you, Trixie!"

His voice was drowned out by the roar of the other race cars speeding past.

"No time, Speed!" said Trixie. She jumped into the passenger seat of the Mach 5. "We've

got a race to win!"

"You're right—as usual," muttered Speed, jumping into the driver's seat.

He threw the Mach 5 into gear, and with a squeal of tires, they were back in the race, heading up the mountain toward Danger Pass!

The Three Roses cars sped faster and faster up the winding road to Danger Pass. They were under orders—to win at any cost.

They soon caught up with the leaders of the race, who weren't expecting foul play.

"Get ready. We'll start knocking some of the other cars out of the race," said one of the Three Roses drivers.

"Let's do it!" said another.

"Here goes!" said the third, as he rammed the bumper of one of the lead cars, sending it into a spin. His partner in crime weaved from side to side, knocking two other cars into the guardrails.

The first victim spun into a boulder and crashed, while the second two smashed through the guardrails and disappeared over the cliff.

All of the Three Roses drivers smiled. Now they were in the lead!

They thought they were safe.

They didn't see the Mélange, two turns behind, catching up with them.

"Hahaha!" Flash cackled. "Soon they will get what they are dishing out to others!"

Meanwhile, Lily was passed out at the wheel. As the Mélange careened around the sharp curves, racing to catch up with the Three Roses cars, Flash shouted into the radio mike:

"Lily! Can you hear me? Lily, wake up! It's me, Flash. You'll be in Danger Pass soon—time to avenge our father! Lily, we're going to get them!"

Speed was following far behind, taking the curves on two wheels, making up for lost time. Trixie was right beside him, in the passenger seat.

He pointed at the helicopter ahead and above. "I believe Flash Junior is up there, operating car number three by remote control! That's Lily at the wheel."

"Oh!" said Trixie. "You mean car number three is really the Mélange?"

"That's what I think," said Speed. "And I think he's out for revenge! If we don't stop him, he will wreck all the Three Roses cars, and maybe more besides!"

"We're out of radio range," said Trixie. "I'll use the homing robot to inform Inspector Detector."

She downloaded a voice message into the Mach 5's homing robot. This was one of the many secret features of the Mach 5.

"Car number three is really the Mélange, and it's being operated from a helicopter by remote control," said Trixie. "Lily Marker is at the wheel.

She is in danger! We're approaching the Danger Pass area, and we need your help."

"Go, robot!" said Speed. He pressed the G button at the center of the Mach 5's steering wheel.

A slot opened in the front of the car, and out flew a rocket shaped like a homing pigeon. It circled twice, getting its bearings, and then streaked out of sight.

The race was now at Danger Pass, high in the mountains, far above the clouds. Snowy peaks loomed over the racetrack. The air was thin, the narrow track was steep, the curves were sharp—and so were the rocks below.

The Three Roses cars were in the lead, running in a wedge-shaped pack.

They didn't yet see the X-3 closing in from behind. They didn't see Flash's helicopter, directing it from above.

"At last! Here we are at Danger Pass, and now I'm going to take care of the Three Roses team," Flash said. He pressed the joystick forward on the remote, and the X-3 approached the cars.

Its horn honked: an eerie *BEEP BEEP BEEP.*

The Three Roses drivers heard the sound and looked into their rearview mirrors. What they saw terrified them. They screamed into their radios:

"Now it says X-3!" said one.

"That's the Mélange!" said the other.

"Or its ghost!" said the third.

🌀　🌀　🌀　🌀

It was time for the final revenge. Flash wanted to share the thrill with his sister. "Lily, wake up! Now is the time. Now we can get revenge for our father!"

Lily finally managed to open her eyes. The car was speeding faster than ever. Above, she could see the red helicopter.

"No, Flash!" she cried. "Please don't go through with it!"

The answer came with a sudden lurch, as Flash rammed the Mélange into one of the Three Roses cars, slamming it toward the loose gravel at the edge of the track.

"Aaah!" cried the driver as his wheels lost traction. His car rolled over and crashed down the mountainside.

"One down!" Flash cried triumphantly as the driver crawled out of the wreck and the car burst into flames.

"You've done enough, Flash!" cried Lily. "Please, stop!"

She turned the wheel desperately and hit the brakes, trying to stop, but the Mélange sped on. It was in Flash's control, not hers.

She heard his voice over the radio: "Two more to go, Lily!"

The two remaining Three Roses drivers saw the wreck, and then the Mélange coming after them. They knew what was in store for them.

"I'm sorry," said one. "I was just following orders!"

"Don't wreck me," said the other. "Show some mercy, please!"

Flash heard their cries from overhead. "Mercy?" He laughed. He didn't know the meaning of the word. With the remote control, he crashed the Mélange into the second Three Roses car,

sending it into a spin.

"Aaah!" wailed the driver as his car careened off the rocks and landed upside down in the canyon below. A battered driver crawled out of the ruined race car.

Lily held on for dear life and screamed into the radio. "Please, Flash! You've done enough damage!"

"Not yet, Lily," Flash muttered in answer. "One more to go!"

Still racing to catch up, Speed and Trixie saw both crashes from the Mach 5.

"I'm too late!" Speed said. "I've got to do something to stop him."

"Oh, Speed," said Trixie. "Be careful!"

The Mélange and the last Three Roses driver were too far ahead. The switchback curves of Danger Pass were too tight. Even the Mach 5 couldn't get through them in time to prevent another tragedy.

But Speed knew that the Mach 5 had a secret

weapon. Pops had added it for emergencies—and this was an emergency!

"Hang on, Trixie!" he said.

He pressed the B button on the steering wheel, and a special traction tread extended over the tires. With the added traction, he steered off the racetrack, across the icy face of a glacier.

"Oh!" cried Trixie.

Taking full advantage of his added traction, Speed sped across the smooth ice, and then up a rocky cliff, back onto the racetrack.

He smiled. The shortcut had worked, and now he was in between the two lead cars!

From the helicopter, Flash saw the Mach 5 as it cut across the ice and then slipped back onto the track between the Mélange and the last of the Three Roses cars.

Now Flash's victim was out of reach!

"What!" he shouted. "The Mach 5? How dare he get in my way."

Screaming with rage, he opened the

emergency rescue kit and pulled out a flare gun. It fired bright rockets, like roman candles. They were distress signals, designed to help, not hurt.

But they could hurt at close range!

Flash flew lower toward the ground and opened the helicopter door.

"Oh!" cried Trixie as she looked up and saw the flare gun in Flash's hand.

"No sweat," said Speed. "Pops has prepared the Mach 5 for just such an attack."

Speed hit another button on his steering wheel. This one closed the cockpit, covering it with an impenetrable canopy of clear Plexiglas.

The flares bounced off harmlessly.

Above, Flash was furious. He worked the remote, trying to get around Speed so he could wreck the last Three Roses car.

No good! Speed blocked his every move.

He tried to crash the Mélange into the Mach 5, but Speed dodged him expertly.

Flash roared with rage, his cries lost in the

roar of engines below. Meanwhile, on a towering mountain above the pass, a snowfield shook, loosened by the blast of the helicopter's rotors.

The snow began to slide, faster and faster, down toward the narrow racetrack.

Trixie screamed as she looked up through the Plexiglas windshield. All she could see was snow.

Then there was a sound like thunder, and everything went white.

Avalanche!

Silence.

Everything was still.

Trixie and Speed looked at each other in the dim light.

The Mach 5 was buried.

"We've got to get out of here before all our oxygen is used up," said Trixie.

"Right as usual," said Speed. "Let's try to climb out."

He pressed a button, and the Plexiglas canopy slid open.

Cold snow poured down on Trixie's head. Speed laughed and started to climb up through the snow, digging as he went.

"What's so funny," muttered Trixie. She tried to follow Speed as he tunneled up through the snow, slipping and sliding.

She was just about to run out of breath when

she saw daylight above. And Speed's smile!

"Come on, give me your hand," he said, pulling her up to daylight. "We're safe now!"

"That's what you think!" said a cold voice, even colder than the snow.

It was Flash.

The helicopter was parked on the snow, with the Mélange right beside it. Lily was in the race car, looking dazed.

"I get rid of everybody who gets in my way, and that's what you did, Speed. Now I'm going to take care of you and your girlfriend."

"You'll never get away with it," said Speed. "The police will be here any minute."

"You will be toast by the time they get here," cried Flash, swinging his crutch like a bat as he lunged at Speed.

"No, Flash!" shouted Lily. She threw herself at Flash, knocking him down. Speed ran at Flash, fists clenched—then stopped when he heard a distant rumble getting closer and closer.

It was another avalanche, triggered by their shouts!

A wall of snow swept down the mountain as Flash and Speed, Trixie and Lily all started running. But they couldn't outrun the snow. In a matter of seconds, they were all enveloped in a cloud of loose snow.

Trixie and Lily struggled to their feet. Flash, looking dazed, was on his knees beside them.

Trixie looked around. "Speed, where are you?"

She looked in every direction. Speed was

nowhere to be seen. The avalanche must have buried him!

"Your precious Speed Racer is gone!" said Flash. With an evil laugh, he grabbed his crutch and started for the helicopter. "That avalanche finished him off for good!"

"Oh, no!" cried Trixie.

"Flash, wait!" cried Lily. "Don't leave me here!"

Flash ignored her. He got into the helicopter and the rotors started to spin, slowly at first, then faster and faster.

"Now to finish my revenge," he said as he

lifted off the snow. "There is one more Three Roses car left!"

He flew off, leaving Lily and Trixie standing side by side. Beside them, the Mélange roared to life and sped off. This time there was no one in the driver's seat. Flash was driving it by remote control.

Trixie and Lily looked at each other. They were alone. Each was about to burst into tears, when—

Trixie saw a hand emerge from the snow. Then another.

"Speed!" she said as he crawled out of the snow and collapsed. "You've been hurt!"

Speed's arm was bleeding where a jagged sheet of ice had scratched it.

"He's freezing!" said Lily. Speed groaned and fell down on the snow. His eyes were closed.

"I'm going to get a first aid kit!" said Trixie. Luckily, the Mach 5 had been partially uncovered by the second avalanche.

"If he isn't kept warm, he won't pull through," said Lily. "I've got to keep him warm!"

Lily lay down and took Speed in her arms. Her tears fell on his face. "I'm sorry," she sobbed. "I'm sorry for what my brother, Flash, has done to you and the others!"

"Huh?" Trixie came running with the first aid kit from the Mach 5. She stopped when she saw Lily holding Speed in her arms.

"Get away!" Trixie knocked Lily aside and put her own arms around Speed.

"Come on!" she cried. "You've got to pull out of it. Wake up, Speed! Can't you hear me?"

Speed opened his eyes and smiled. "Trixie?"

"Who else?" she responded.

Meanwhile, a convoy of police vehicles was climbing up Danger Pass. They had gotten the message from the robot drone.

Pops Racer and Sparky were riding in the lead vehicle with Inspector Detector. Spritle and Chim Chim had been left behind—or so Pops thought.

"I never suspected Flash Marker Junior was behind this whole plot," said Inspector Detector. "It was clever of Speed to make the discovery. He's a smart boy."

"Well, after all, he's a chip off the old block!" said Pops. "He gets his smarts from me!"

"What about the other chip, Pops?" said Sparky. "Does Spritle get his mischief from you, too?"

"Well, uh—" Pops began.

"Yes!" said a tiny voice. Pops looked down and saw Spritle and Chim Chim, hiding under the seat.

"You rascals!" said Pops, dragging them out. "Stowed away again, huh?"

"Right, Pops. Chip off old block," said Spritle.

"Woo-hoo," agreed Chim Chim.

They all laughed as the convoy sped on toward Danger Pass. Even Inspector Detector.

On the mountaintop, Lily was still sobbing. "I'm sorry all this happened because of my brother!" she said.

"Don't cry, Lily," Trixie said. "You're not to blame for the terrible things your brother has done."

"And is still doing!" said Speed. He was feeling better, and he was anxious to get moving. "The important thing is to finish digging out the Mach 5 and catch up to the Mélange before your brother strikes again."

"All right, Speed," said Lily, wiping the

from her blue eyes. "Thanks for those kind words. Just tell me what I can do to be of help."

"Start digging," said Trixie.

"Right as usual," said Speed. "Let's dig the Mach 5 out of the snow and get it started. We had better hurry! Who knows where the Mélange could be right now?"

"Or what my brother will try next!" said Lily.

Leaving the avalanche far behind, the Mélange raced to catch up with the last of the Three Roses cars. The road ahead was clear of snow.

Overhead, in the helicopter, Flash was working the remote and grinning with anticipation. "Only one more to get rid of! Then my revenge will be complete."

Finally, the Mach 5 was back in action, with Speed at the wheel and Trixie close beside him. Lily had stayed behind to wait for the police.

The mighty engine roared as Speed negotiated the switchbacks of Danger Pass. The speedometer read 240, the fastest he had ever gone!

He sped into a tunnel without slowing, skillfully avoiding the rock walls. A boulder, loosened by the avalanche, blocked the way! Speed used his hydraulic auto jacks to leap over

the boulder and sped on.

Trixie pointed up ahead. "There's the helicopter!"

"We must be near the Mélange," said Speed. "Hang on!"

Trixie hung on happily. She was never afraid when Speed was at the wheel.

Flash looked down from the helicopter and frowned. "The Mach 5 again! So, I didn't get rid of Speed Racer after all."

The Mélange sped across a bridge spanning a cold, icy river. The Mach 5 followed a few moments later.

Then they rounded a sharp curve.

"There's the Mélange!" shouted Trixie. It was just ahead.

"I don't want to wreck it," said Speed, unfastening his seat belt. "I have another plan."

"You do?"

"You'll have to drive the Mach 5, Trixie. Don't be scared."

Trixie's eyes were wide with horror. Speed was climbing out his window, onto the car's hood!

"But I am scared!" Trixie yelled.

"This is no time for fear, Trixie! Take the wheel!"

Trixie summoned all her courage and slid into the driver's seat.

Surprising even herself, she drove skillfully until the Mach 5 was side by side with the driverless Mélange.

"Good driving!" shouted Speed as he jumped from the Mach 5 into the empty Mélange.

He took the wheel and spun it, left and right. The car didn't respond. He tried the brakes. They didn't work, either.

"I have to find the remote control!" he said. "Once I disconnect it, I will be in control of the car."

The radio crackled. Flash had been listening. "No time, Speed. I'm in control."

Speed looked ahead. The last Three Roses car was only a few car lengths ahead on the narrow road. Speed looked under the seat, then under the dash. No luck!

"The remote control receiver has to be somewhere in the car, but where?"

He lurched from side to side as Flash made the car weave, trying to throw him out. He tried the wheel again.

It came off in his hands!

"Hahaha," laughed Flash over the radio. "You haven't much time, Speed!"

The driver of the Three Roses car was looking over his shoulder. His eyes were wide with terror. "The Mélange is after me!" he cried. "Help!"

"You don't deserve it," muttered Speed. "But I will try."

Speed had one last idea where the remote receiver might be. He climbed over the windshield.

The 200 mph wind almost blew him off the car. He gripped the hood with his fingertips and held on for dear life.

"Careful, Speed, you're liable to hurt yourself out there!" Flash's voice on the radio sounded gleeful. He was having fun!

The road narrowed over a high cliff. Below was the icy river.

The Mélange was closing in on the Three Roses car, about to ram it, and Speed Racer was helpless. But he had to keep looking for that remote receiver.

With a mighty effort, he pulled the hood open. Underneath, on top of the engine, he saw a bundle of wires leading to a black box.

The remote receiver!

He ripped out the wires just as the Mélange nudged the side of the Three Roses car, sending it into a sideways skid.

"Aaah!" screamed the driver. He jumped free just before the car went over the cliff.

Above, Flash worked the joystick in panic, but it did no good. The remote was disconnected, and the Mélange was spinning out of control.

Speed held onto the hood for dear life. Then he felt the car crash against the guardrail.

Then he felt weightless, as he and the Mélange soared through the air, toward the river far below.

In the helicopter far above, Flash watched the Mélange crash through the guardrail and fall into the icy water. He crushed the useless remote control in his hands.

Angry tears streamed down his face. "Oh, no, the Mélange! My father's beautiful car has been wrecked. What have I done?"

He had finally gotten his revenge. But it had cost him his soul.

The Mach 5, with Trixie at the wheel, and the police caravan screeched to a halt on the track. They ran to the broken guardrail and looked down. Lily was with them.

"Speed! Speed!" they all cried.

There was no answer. They saw only the burning Three Roses car and the rushing river where the Mélange had drowned.

The only movement was the helicopter, which was flying over the chasm, spinning from side to side like an angry bee. Then it swooped upward and disappeared over a distant mountain peak.

"Flash! Come back!" cried Lily.

But he was gone.

Meanwhile, Trixie was crying. "Speed! Oh, Speed!" she wailed. Heedless of her own safety, she ran down the steep slope toward the river, jumping from rock to rock.

"No one, not even Speed, could have survived that crash," said Sparky, fighting back his own tears as he ran after her. Inspector Detector and Pops Racer followed more slowly, picking their way through the jagged boulders.

Behind them, Spritle was wailing, *"Waaaaah!"*

Chim Chim joined in.

"I'm the one to blame for losing Speed," said Inspector Detector gloomily. "I had no one else to turn to and we badly needed help. I should never have asked him to do it."

"I wish there had never been a Mélange," said Pops. "I wish I had never heard of racing!"

Trixie sat down on the riverbank. She had never felt so lost and so alone.

Then she heard splashing behind her.

She turned and saw a familiar figure swimming toward her. He was shivering with cold—but smiling!

"It's Speed!"

He reached the shore just as Trixie, Pops, Spritle, and Chim Chim all ran to greet him and hug him. They knocked him back, and they all fell into the water together.

Then they climbed out, laughing and shivering.

"Glad you're safe, Speed," said Inspector Detector when they were all back on shore.

"So are we all," said Pops.

"We thought you were done for!" said Sparky.

"The Mélange is gone forever," said Speed Racer as he gave Trixie a big hug. "But surely you all knew I would be okay!"

Then they heard sobbing.

Lily was sitting on a boulder, all alone. She was looking toward the distant ridge where her brother had disappeared.

"I know I will never see him again," she wailed. "Flash is too ashamed of what he has done. He is gone forever."

Good riddance, thought Speed. But he knew better than to say it.

"I remember when my brother was little. He was such a good boy," Lily said with a sob. "Too bad he had to change."

"It was the desire for revenge that did it," said Speed.

"Always remember him when he was little and forget the way he turned out," said Trixie. She took Lily's hand and led her up the hill to the waiting cars. "I just want you to know that Speed and I will always be your friends."

"Oh, will you?" Lily cried. "I'd like that more than anything else in the world! And I hope that someday maybe you and everyone else in the world will forgive Flash."

She wiped away her tears—then followed Speed and his family and friends into a brighter future.

The Danger Pass race was a DNF (did not finish) for the Mach 5 and me. But that was okay. I knew I would be able to try again the next year.

Flash Marker was not so lucky.

I felt sorry for what had happened to him. He wasn't all bad. The desire for revenge had twisted him and caused him to do evil. But in his own misguided way, he did it out of love. Perhaps, if things had worked out differently, we might even have been friends. I wish I'd had the chance to compete against Flash in a fair race, where he was trying to win instead of just racing for revenge.

Danger Pass reminds me of another race where I was trying to stop another man who was consumed with hatred. But his story turned out differently. He was able to learn his lesson before it was too late.

It all started with a drive in the country . . .

The Car Hater
One: Reckless Drivers

The Mach 5 sped through the countryside. The powerful engine roared, making a beautiful sound. The tires sang as they gripped the curves.

140, 150 mph! Speed Racer was nervous. And no wonder. He wasn't driving. He was in the passenger seat!

"I love taking the wheel," said Trixie, Speed's girlfriend. "Thanks for letting me drive."

"Take it easy," said Speed. "The speed limit here is only 80 mph!"

Trixie slowed down. "I didn't realize we were going twice that fast!"

Speed checked the rearview mirror. He saw a car coming up fast. He didn't want to get a ticket. But it wasn't the police. It was a convertible, and it was weaving from side to side.

"A reckless driver!" he said.

The convertible was filled with teenage boys.

They pulled alongside the Mach 5 and taunted Trixie. "You drive just like a girl!"

Trixie tried to outrun them, but they caught up on the curves and smashed into the side of the Mach 5 again and again.

Speed took the wheel to help out. "Stop that!" he yelled. They were denting his precious car!

The reckless teens smashed into the Mach 5 again. Then they lost control and their convertible went into a dangerous spin.

The Mach 5 was just about to plow into them when Speed reached over Trixie and hit a button on the steering wheel, extending the Mach 5's auto jacks.

The sleek race car flew into the air, barely avoiding the skidding convertible. As soon as the wheels were back on the ground, Trixie hit the brakes.

They pulled to a stop. "That was a close call!" said Speed.

"It sure was!" said Speed's little brother, Spritle, as he popped out of the trunk. He and his pet chimpanzee, Chim Chim, were always stowing away somewhere.

Just then the reckless teens pulled up alongside the Mach 5. They jumped out of the convertible with wrenches and tire irons. "Let's mess up their car!" they said.

"Oh, yeah?" Speed was just about to take them on when the teens stopped suddenly. "This is the Mach 5!" one said.

"And that's Speed Racer!" said another.

Soon, instead of fighting, they were asking for Speed's autograph!

Two: Hot Stuff

Later that afternoon, Speed was in a soda shop with the teens, giving them advice on driving.

"A racer is never reckless," he said, wanting them to know how dangerous their driving earlier in the day had been.

But little did they know that a group of thugs was nearby, listening. The thugs were envious of Speed. They thought he was a show-off.

"Think you're hot stuff?" they asked Speed.

Speed tried to ignore them. But the thugs were determined to cause trouble. They attacked with bottles, chairs, and fists. Speed knocked them out, while the teens looked on admiringly.

"Had enough?" Speed asked, "or would you like some more?"

"No more!" cried the thugs as they crawled away, out the door.

The teens all laughed and Speed went back to giving them advice and telling them racing stories.

Three: Weapons

Trixie was bored. She had heard most of Speed's stories.

She looked outside the soda shop and saw a pretty girl admiring the Mach 5.

Sprite was showing her the controls, while Chim Chim looked on.

Trixie joined them and introduced herself. The girl's name was Janine. "This is a fabulous car," she said. "I would like to be a race car driver someday, but my father will never let me. He hates cars!"

Trixie had an idea. "Would you like to drive the Mach 5 around the block?"

"Would I!"

With Janine at the wheel, they started around

the block. Suddenly they heard hoof beats. A man on a horse came around the corner.

The Mach 5's engine spooked the horse, and it began to buck. Speed ran out to help. The rider was thrown off.

Janine ran to him. "Papa!"

As Janine's father, Mr. Trotter, looked up at his daughter, his eyes flashed with rage. "Janine! You were driving that car! I told you never to drive a car!"

He stood up and began to kick the Mach 5. "I hate cars!" he cried. "All cars are weapons on wheels. I hate them. They should be destroyed."

Speed Racer tried to calm him down. "When they're driven right, they are perfectly safe!"

"Don't tell me that!" raged Mr. Trotter. "I lost my son in a car accident, and I hate all cars. Janine, I want you to come home right away."

And he jumped on his horse and rode off. With tears in her eyes, Janine followed on foot.

Four: Too Many Accidents!

Later, in the family garage, Speed looked on while Sparky and Pops repaired the dents in the Mach 5. Some were from the teens' convertible, and others were from Mr. Trotter's kicks.

"The paint is scraped completely off," said Pops Racer, shaking his head. "What happened?"

Before Speed could explain, Pops held up a newspaper. There were several headlines about dangerous car accidents.

"You have to be more careful, Speed," he said. "There are too many accidents these days."

Meanwhile, in a mansion across town, the car hater, Mr. Trotter, was reading the same newspaper.

"Too many accidents!" he muttered. "If there were no cars, there would be no accidents. Look here, Janine!"

He handed his daughter the newspaper. She took it without answering. She knew better than to argue with her father about cars.

"Janine, I don't want to catch you around a car again. Do you hear me?"

"Sure," she said. She looked at the back page of the paper and smiled.

"Where are you going?"

"Out, Papa." She walked out the door.

Mr. Trotter picked up the paper and looked at the page his daughter had been reading. BIG RACE TODAY! it said.

Suddenly, Mr. Trotter knew where his daughter had gone. And he knew what he had to do.

Five: Turmoil on the Track

"How's the new track?" Trixie asked as Speed pulled into the pit in the Mach 5. The big race was almost half over.

"Great!" said Speed.

"Hello, Speed!" said a girl's voice. It was Janine!

"What are you doing here?" Trixie asked. "Won't you get in trouble?"

"I can't help it," said Janine. "I love being

around fast cars!"

"Me too," said Sparky, making a quick adjustment to the Mach 5.

Just then, Janine's father rode up on his horse. "I told you, no cars!" he shouted. Janine ducked behind the Mach 5 and burst into tears.

"They shouldn't build racetracks!" Mr. Trotter shouted. He rode his horse out onto the track, into the path of the speeding race cars.

"Stop!" shouted the racing officials. But it was too late. Tires screamed as the race cars jammed on their brakes, trying not to hit the horse and rider.

The lead cars spun out, and the rest of the

cars piled into them. The noise was deafening. The track was filled with twisted metal. Dazed drivers sat in their wrecked cars. It was a catastrophe.

Mr. Trotter looked on, pleased. "There," he said. "That gets rid of some cars!"

Mr. Trotter rode off, triumphantly. Police and racing officials tried to follow, but they were stopped by an oil drum that had been rolled down the grandstand stairs by three thugs—the same thugs Speed had worked over in the soda shop.

"We hate cars, too," they told Mr. Trotter. "And we need a job."

Mr. Trotter tossed them a business card with his address. "Come see me tonight," he said. "I think we might be able to work together."

Six: Dirty Work

That evening, the car hater met with the three thugs. "We must show everyone how dangerous cars are," Mr. Trotter said. He gave the thugs their

orders—and a stack of cash.

Just then the phone rang. It was his daughter. "I'm not coming home," she said, "not until you change your mind about cars."

"Where are you, Janine?" he asked. The answer was a click. She had hung up!

Janine wiped away a tear and turned to her new friends.

"Maybe it would be best if you stayed with us for a while," said Trixie.

"Oh, thank you, I will!" said Janine.

That night the three thugs broke into car dealerships all over town. They went to work: loosening lug nuts, cutting brake lines, and unscrewing steering gears.

The next day started with a bang. Then another bang, and another, as runaway cars crashed though windows, ran stoplights, lost their wheels, and caught on fire!

The thugs cackled gleefully. They were making money—and having fun! Their next target would be the race cars!

In his mansion, Mr. Trotter watched the news with pleasure. No one could trace the chaos to him! Soon all the cars would be destroyed, and his daughter would return.

Meanwhile, Janine was enjoying riding around with her new friends. She and Trixie were on their way downtown when they were stopped by a cop. "Too many crashes," he said. "No more cars allowed in the city."

They went to a soda shop and saw it all on TV. Because of the accidents, traffic was hopelessly snarled.

Janine had a sinking feeling. Could someone be deliberately causing these accidents?

She was afraid she knew the answer.

Seven: Caught in the Act

The next day, Speed and Sparky were returning from a test drive in the Mach 5. Spritle and Chim Chim were in the back seat.

"Hey," said Sparky as they approached the garage. "Didn't I just see three shadows sneaking across the road and into the garage?"

"I'll bet they are the ones causing all these

crashes," said Speed.

They sneaked in and surprised them. Once Speed had the leader of the thugs flattened on the floor, he asked, "Who are you working for?"

The answer didn't surprise him.

Speed and Sparky immediately hauled the thugs to the Trotter mansion.

"No use lying, Mr. Trotter," said Speed. "We know you are behind all these terrible accidents."

"Get out of here!" said Mr. Trotter. "I admit to nothing. And where is my daughter, Janine?"

"She is with Trixie," said Sparky. "They were taking a drive in a new sports car from Pops Racer's

shop. A red runabout."

The leader of the three thugs, a sneaky little man, gulped. "I worked on that car, Mr. Trotter. I fixed the brakes and the steering both."

"What? My daughter is in danger!"

Mr. Trotter jumped onto his horse and rode off.

Speed jumped into the Mach 5. He had to save Trixie!

Eight: Drive into Danger

It was a perfect day for a drive. Trixie loved the way the new sports car handled. It had plenty of power for climbing the steep grades of the Craggy Peak Mountains.

But when they reached the top and started down the long twisted road, she saw what it was missing.

"We have no brakes!" she cried.

"Try the emergency brake!" shouted Janine.

She did.

No good!

The car went faster and faster down the steep grade!

⊕ ⊕ ⊕ ⊕

Speed caught up with Mr. Trotter near the top of the mountain road.

He pulled over and said, "Get in, Mr. Trotter. You'll never catch up with them on that horse."

Mr. Trotter glared down at him. "After my son was killed, I swore never to ride in a car," he said.

He spurred the horse and galloped off.

Speed gunned the Mach 5 and followed, in search of Trixie and Janine.

Faster and faster the sabotaged sports car went. It was careening out of control down the steep mountain road.

Trixie pumped the useless brakes. She watched the speedometer in terror.

180 mph, 190 mph—

In the rearview mirror, she saw Speed in the Mach 5, trying to catch up. "Hurry, Speed!" she cried. "Help us, if you can!"

The road narrowed and the turns were even tighter. Now the car was going almost 200 mph!

WHAM, WHAM!

Janine and Trixie screamed as the car smashed off the cliffs, spinning from side to side.

The car crashed through the guardrail. It turned over in the air and fell onto the rocks below.

"Trixie!" cried Speed.

When Speed got to the wreck, he saw that Trixie was still inside. Her seat belt had saved her. She was dazed but okay.

"Help Janine," she said, pointing to a crumpled figure lying on the ground nearby.

Speed ran over and picked up Janine. She was unconscious. "We have to get her to a hospital!" he cried.

Just then Mr. Trotter rode up. He jumped off his horse and grabbed his injured daughter from Speed. "I will take her," he said. "She's my daughter."

He tried to climb back onto the horse with Janine, but the horse was worn out from running. It sank to the ground, exhausted.

"That horse won't get her to the hospital in time," said Speed. "Please, Mr. Trotter, let me take her in the Mach 5!"

Mr. Trotter hesitated.

Trixie spoke up angrily. "We don't care how much you hate cars," she said. "Janine's

life is more important!"

Mr. Trotter gave up. He handed his daughter back to Speed Racer. He watched, with a tear in his eye, as Speed and Trixie put her into the Mach 5 and raced off.

Nine: A Lesson Learned

A few weeks later, there was a small party in a nearby hospital room.

Janine Trotter was recovered from her injuries. It was finally time for her to go home.

Her new friends, Trixie, Speed, Sparky, and Pops Racer were gathered in her room.

"Oh, thank you!" she said when Spritle and Chim Chim gave her flowers.

Then she heard a deep voice behind her. "Janine! My daughter!" Her father came racing through the door.

"Papa!" she cried. She threw her arms around him. "Why have you waited so long to come and see me in the hospital?"

"I've been in jail," said Mr. Trotter. "Paying for my crimes. But I have learned my lesson. I can see now that a car can be either a weapon or a lifesaver, depending on who is driving."

"That's good," said Pops Racer. "I brought you a present. It's even better than a horse—and it never gets tired."

He showed Mr. Trotter the car he had built especially for him. It was a new convertible!

That afternoon, they all went for a drive. "Thank you all," said Mr. Trotter. "Janine, I've thought about it a lot—and I have decided to let you be a race car driver, if that's what you want!"

"Oh, thank you, Papa!" she said.

"Speed can teach you to drive safely," said Trixie.

"What about those thugs you hired?" asked Speed.

"I put them to work doing good," said Mr. Trotter. "I wanted to make up for all the wrecks I caused."

He pointed to the side of the road.

One of the thugs was helping an old lady across the street. Another was clumsily directing traffic. They were doing their best to do some good.

Speed Racer smiled. The car hater had learned his lesson. Traffic was running smoothly again. At least for now!

Racing to DVD
May 2008

Classic Speed Racer DVDs
Also Available!